Tough Stuff

Tough Stuff

Shannon White

RESOURCE *Publications* · Eugene, Oregon

Resource Publications
A division of Wipf and Stock Publishers
199 W 8th Ave, Suite 3
Eugene, OR 97401

Tough Stuff
By White, Shannon
Copyright©2016 by White, Shannon
ISBN 13: 978-1-5326-9205-5
Publication date 5/17/2019
Previously published by Tate Publishing, 2016

Contents

Introduction

You are young!

You are smart!

You are full of potential!

You are going to do great things in your life!

You have a lot of great qualities!

You believe in God!

You are saved!

...And you live in this world full of temptations and struggles. NOW WHAT!

SOMETIMES BEING SAVED and young is easy. Sometimes it can be tough. The most important thing is that you ARE saved and that is amazing! The Bible says if you declare with your mouth, "Jesus is Lord," and believe in your heart that God raised him from the dead, you will be saved (Romans 10:9, NIV)! It's that simple! But a lot of times, adults forget how challenging it can be as a saved young person!

You may have school pressure, peer pressure, parent pressure, and self-pressure to do the right things or be your best while you also have to juggle pressure and temptations to do the wrong things.

God loves that you are saved and young because you are strong, have energy, and can do great things. In the Bible, Paul encourages you not to let anyone look down on you because you are young, but to set an example for the believers in speech (how you talk), in conduct (how you behave), in love (how you show love), in faith (how you show you trust in God) and in purity (how you live holy) (1 Timothy 4:12, NIV). This means God charges you, as a young person, to be an example to your friends, family, teachers, parents, and all other believers in Christ. Yes, it does sound like a big job, but it can be done, even at your young age!

If you don't believe me, let's look at the Bible.

King Josiah was made king when he was only 8 years old, and he did so many great things to honor God.

King Joash was made king when he was only 7 years old, and he also did good things to show honor to God and be an example.

David was only a teenager when he killed Goliath and helped save Israel.

These are just some examples that it is possible to be a follower of Christ while you are young. So many other young people are living saved, and so can you!

The good part is that when Jesus went back to heaven after dying on the cross, God sent the comforter, the Holy

Spirit, to help you make good choices. His job is to help teach you and help you remember everything God has said to you. So, you have back up to help you stay saved and young, even when things get tough!

THE TOUGH NEWS IS THIS:

> Your enemy, the devil, prowls around like a roaring lion looking for someone to devour. (1 Pet. 5:8, NIV)

This means that the devil is looking for someone to destroy, including young people like you!

THE GOOD NEWS IS THIS:

> Jesus has given you authority to trample on snakes and scorpions and to overcome all the power of the enemy; nothing will harm you. (Lk. 10:18, NIV)

Because

> We can call on God, and he will answer us; He will be with us in trouble, He will deliver and honor us. (Ps. 91:15, NIV)

Because

> God knows the plans he has for you, plans to prosper you and not to harm you, plans to give you a hope and a future. (Jer. 29:11, NIV)

So

> You can do all things through Christ that strengthens you. (Phil. 4:13, NIV)

The tough stuff is all around you! This book is to help you remember the word and promises of God when you are living your life. It's a cheat code to help you remember to keep it saved and young! You don't have to be boring and saved. Jesus came so that we could have an abundant life! So enjoy being young, but remember to make decisions that will make our Heavenly Father proud!

You can keep this book in your pencil pouch, your locker, your purse, your car, or even download it to your electronic device! This is about helping you get through the tough stuff, staying saved and young, and enjoying your life!

So here are some topics that you can study and learn about to remind you what God has to say about them.

The truth is that sometimes you may find yourself alone, at school, or with friends and need a moment to check what the Bible says about a situation you are having. After all, you are saved and young and still learning how to live as a kingdom kid!

A

❖ Abuse

- *The LORD is a refuge for the oppressed, a stronghold in times of trouble (Psalm 9:9, NIV).*

    o **What does it mean to me?**

    The Lord is my safe place if I am hurting or crushed and in my times of trouble. I he is are with me so I lean on him for help. He keeps me safe!

    o **Your quick prayer:**

    I am hurting and crushed. Thank you, Lord, for being my safe place in this time of trouble.

- *In my distress, I called to the LORD; I cried to my God for help. From his temple, he heard my voice; my cry came before him, into his ears (Psalm 18:6, NIV).*

    o **What does it mean to me?**

    When I am in trouble I can call to the Lord. I can cry to God for help. From his temple he will hear my voice; my cry will come to his ears.

○ **Your quick prayer:**

> God I am in trouble. I am calling you, God, for help. Thank you for hearing my voice and listening when I cry to you! Show me what to do!

❖ Anal Sex (See *Sex*)

❖ Anxiety

- *Do not be anxious about anything, but in every situation, by prayer and petition, with thanksgiving, present your requests to God. And the peace of God, which transcends all understanding, will guard your hearts and your minds in Christ Jesus (Philippians 4:6-7, NIV).*

    ○ **What does it mean to me?**

    > I do not have to let anything make me anxious or distracted because in every situation, with prayer and asking, with giving thanks, I can give my requests to God. Then God's peace, which is bigger than my thinking, will protect my heart and mind in Christ Jesus.

    ○ **Your quick prayer:**

    > I will not let this make me anxious *or* nervous! God thank you for being with me and being in

control of everything! Father, I love you and am asking for your help with_____ (Fill in the blank for your situation). I trust you when you said you will be with me, and thank you for your peace. I receive your peace now in Jesus's name.

❖ Arguments

- *A gentle answer turns away wrath, but a harsh word stirs up anger (Proverbs 15:1, NIV).*

  ○ **What does it mean to me?**

  > Giving someone a nice response turns away wrath and arguments, but using hurtful or mean words brings more anger and arguments.

  ○ **Your quick prayer:**

  > Father, show me how to give a gentle answer so I can stop this argument. Help me understand where the other person is coming from.

- *Keep reminding God's people of these things. Warn them before God against quarreling about words; it is of no value, and only ruins those who listen (2 Timothy 2:14, NIV).*

  ○ **What does it mean to me?**

  > As God's child, he wants me to remember that fighting with my words is useless. It only destroys those who listen to arguing.

  ○ **Your quick prayer:**

  > Father, show me what to say. Let my words be helpful and not hurtful to the people that hear them.

❖ Assertiveness

- *"I am sending you out like sheep among wolves. Therefore be as shrewd as snakes and as innocent as doves (Matthew 10:16).*

  - **What does it mean to me?**

    In this world, there are many people who are cruel or mean. Therefore, as a Kingdom Kid, God wants me to be wise but use it for good. He wants me to be smart in what I do but do not aim to hurt people.

  - **Your quick prayer:**

    Father, teach me to be as wise as a serpent and harmless as a dove, so I make you proud with my actions.

❖ Attitude

- *By their fruit you will recognize them. Do people pick grapes from thornbushes, or figs from thistles? (Matthew 7:16,* NIV*).*

  - **What does it mean to me?**

    My actions and attitude will show people if I am a Christian. If I am a Christian, I will act like Christ.

○ **Your quick prayer:**

Lord, let my attitude and actions represent you well today. Let the words of my mouth and the things in my heart become acceptable to you. You are my strength and redeemer (Psalm 19:14, NIV).

• *But we have the mind of Christ (1 Corinthians 2:16b, NIV).*

○ **What does it mean to me?**

I, as a Christian, can have the same attitude of Christ.

○ **Your quick prayer:**

Lord, I am your child. Help me to see things and people through your eyes and not only through my emotions and attitude.

B

❖ Body Image

- *I praise you because I am fearfully and wonderfully made; your works are wonderful, I know that full well (Psalm 139:14, NIV).*

  ○ **What does it mean to me?**

  I praise God because I am awesomely made and set apart by him. I know that God makes wonderful things including me!

  ○ **Your quick prayer:**

  Father, thank you for making me precious in your eyes! Please help me to remember that you made me just the way that I am! Despite everything around me, you knew me and formed me in my mom's belly to be just who I am. I am just right and special like I am!

❖ Breakups

- *The LORD is close to the brokenhearted and saves those who are crushed in spirit (Psalm 34:18, NIV).*

  - **What does it mean to me?**

    God will not leave me alone when I am feeling hurt and crushed. He is even with me in my breakup when I am hurt and embarrassed.

  - **Your quick prayer:**

    God, you promised to be close to those that have broken hearts. I need you to help heal my heart. Thank you for always loving me and never leaving me. I can always count on you!

❖ Bullying/Harassment

- *You prepare a table before me in the presence of my enemies. You anoint my head with oil; my cup overflows (Psalm 23:5, NIV).*

  - **What does it mean to me?**

    In the biblical days, kings would set up a table or a feast for people they cared about. As God's child, he cares about me and will set up good things for me in the very face of my enemies or those that do me harm.

○ **Your quick prayer:**

> Father, even when people treat me wrong, I thank you for preparing good things for me! I know that you said payback belongs to you so help me to let my light shine until you prove yourself and come to my rescue!

• *Do not take revenge, my dear friends, but leave room for God's wrath, for it is written: "It is mine to avenge; I will repay," says the Lord (Romans 12:19, NIV).*

○ **What does it mean to me?**

> Do not payback people who do wrong. God will repay them for their wrong. I should show the love of God. Anyone can love their friends, but what impresses God is loving your enemies.

○ **Your quick prayer:**

> Father, show me how to give you room to be God and not to get revenge on my bullies. Teach me how to still give kind words and a positive attitude and bring someone to help me in this tough time. Thank you for caring for me and every detail of my life! I trust you!

C

❖ Church

- *And let us consider how we may spur one another on toward love and good deeds, not giving up meeting together, as some are in the habit of doing, but encouraging one another—and all the more as you see the Day approaching (Hebrews 10:24–25, NIV).*

  - **What does it mean to me?**

    As Kingdom Kids, we should help encourage each other to keep doing good things and stay in the faith. We come to church to stay strong in our faith, because sometimes it can be hard to remain strong when you live in such a crazy world! God has given us leaders to help us stay focused on God and the kingdom so we can grow and help our brothers and sisters in Christ.

  - **Your quick prayer:**

    Father, thank you for setting up your church so that we can help each other and be reminded of how to shine brightly in this world we live in.

❖ **Cliques (See** *Friends***)**

❖ **College**

- *By their fruit you will recognize them. Do people pick grapes from thornbushes, or figs from thistles? (Matthew 7:16, NIV).*

  ○ **What does it mean to me?**

    You can tell people by their fruit or their actions. In the same way, my actions (including doing my work, being on time, being a good student, child, citizen, etc.) show the kind of believer I am. Colleges also look at my fruit (my grades and records) to recognize if I am a good fit for their school so it is important that I start preparing for college now so my habits and reputation will be good.

  ○ **Your quick prayer:**

    Father, show me how to represent you, not just in church, but also in school. I want my grades and how I treat people in school to make you proud so teach me how to get through the tough times and how to let my fruit or actions represent you well!

❖ Confidence

- *I praise you because I am fearfully and wonderfully made; your works are wonderful, I know that full well (Psalm 139:14, NIV).*

  ○ **What does it mean to me?**

    I praise God because I am made by him and set apart by him. I know that God makes wonderful things including me!

  ○ **Your quick prayer:**

    Father, please help me to remember that you made me just the way that I am! Despite everything around me you knew me and took the time to form me in my mom's belly to be just who I am. I can do all things through Christ that strengthens me. Thank you for making me precious in your eyes!

❖ Criticism

- *As iron sharpens iron, so one person sharpens another (Proverbs 27:17, NIV).*

  ○ **What does it mean to me?**

    As Kingdom Kids, only words that help build others up according to what they need should come out of my mouth. Showing God's power is choosing words that help the person listening. It also gives a witness that I choose to be set apart to live for God. The way that I speak should not tear others down, but lift them up and make them better.

- ○ **Your quick prayer:**

  Father, let my words bless others and help them grow. Thank you for sending people to help me grow and mature as your child.

❖ Curse/ Cuss Words

- *Do not let any unwholesome talk come out of your mouths, but only what is helpful for building others up according to their needs, that it may benefit those who listen (Ephesians 4:29, NIV).*

  - ○ **What does it mean to me?**

    The way that I speak should not be the same as somebody who is not saved, or else how will people know the difference between someone who is or is not a kingdom kid? We are set apart.

○ **Your quick prayer:**

> Father, let the words of my mouth and the thoughts of my heart be acceptable in your sight. You are my strength when I want to make the wrong choice. Let my words help others understand how children of God can live.

❖ Cutting

- *No temptation has overtaken you except what is common to mankind. And God is faithful; he will not let you be tempted beyond what you can bear. But when you are tempted, he will also provide a way out so that you can endure it (1 Corinthians 10:13, NIV).*

  ○ **What does it mean to me?**

  > We, as believers, are tempted to do things that could harm us spiritually or naturally. Cutting myself is another temptation when I am having a hard time, but God does not like to see me hurting myself. God loves me so much and he knows there are hard times in life. He is faithful so he will provide a way out of cutting with things like a distraction, a blessing, or a song so that I can get through this hard time. It would be good for me to find someone to help

me get focused when I have the desire to cut myself. I can call them or meet up with them when I have the desire to cut myself.

○ **Your quick prayer:**

Jesus, there are some things that have hurt me and I know I should not cut myself, but the temptation is here! You said that you would make a way of escape, so open my eyes to see the way of escape and grant me your wisdom to stop cutting! My body is your temple so I commit to treating my body with love and care until things change. (Now, go call your accountability partner or find a different activity).

D

❖ Depression

- *"I have told you these things, so that in me you may have peace. In this world you will have trouble. But take heart! I have overcome the world." (John 16:33, NIV)*

  ○ **What does it mean to me?**

  Jesus told us, as believers, that while we live, we will have troubles in life—some bad things will happen. But I can take heart and be confident because Jesus has already overcome every problem in the world and he will be with me.

  ○ **Your quick prayer:**

  Father, I am struggling to be happy. I just feel sad, and I know I am having troubles, but I need your peace. Help me to see things the way you see them and teach me to take heart until things get better.

❖ Drinking

- *Do not get drunk on wine, which leads to debauchery. Instead, be filled with the Spirit (Ephesians 5:18, NIV).*

  - ○ **What does it mean to me?**

    God wants me to be filled with the Holy Spirit and the good things from God. I should not to get drunk from wine or alcohol because it leads to making bad decisions and consequences.

  - ○ **Your quick prayer:**

    Father, when temptation to drink alcohol comes, show me the way of escape and give me courage to take the way that may be unpopular, so that I can let my light shine and stay holy.

❖ Drugs/ Smoking

- *What good is it for someone to gain the whole world, yet forfeit their soul? Or what can anyone give in exchange for their soul? (Matthew 16:26, NIV).*

  ○ **What does it mean to me?**

    I should ask myself: Is this decision I'm making worth giving up my relationship with Christ? Is the popularity, smoking, drinking, money, party, and etc. worth messing up my relationship with God?

  ○ **Your quick prayer:**

    Father, help me to remember that I am a Kingdom Kid and that my body belongs to you. Right now, I choose to work out my own salvation. Nobody can make this choice but me so, God, I choose to be close to you. I know that my body is a temple for your Holy Spirit, and I am choosing not to disrespect your Spirit by putting drugs into my body where your Spirit lives. Lord, I am choosing you over smoking or drugs. Help me to stay strong!

E

❖ Eating Disorder/Disordered Eating

- *Because he himself suffered when he was tempted, he is able to help those who are being tempted (Hebrews 2:18, NIV).*

  - **What does it mean to me?**

    Even if nobody understands—because Jesus also suffered when he was tempted in all things—he is able to help me when I am tempted to use unhealthy eating behaviors.

  - **Your quick prayer:**

    Lord, I am having a hard time. Show me who I am and give me strength when I feel weak. I am wonderfully made by you. You are my safe place and I need your help because I am tempted to _____ (fill in the blank for your situation). Only you can help me through this. Teach me your love so I can love myself.

❖ Enemies

- *Settle matters quickly with your adversary who is taking you to court. Do it while you are still together on the way, or your adversary may hand you over to the judge, and the judge may hand you over to the officer, and you may be thrown into prison (Matthew 5:25, NIV).*

  - **What does it mean to me?**

    I should handle issues quickly with someone who accuses me of something. I should settle my conflicts so my enemy or the person I am having conflict with does not make a bigger issue if it can be quickly handled. I need to let my pride go and reach an agreement to move on with my life.

  - **Your quick prayer:**

    Sometimes people make it hard, but show me how to have gentle words. Father, teach me not to let issues continue with others. If something bad happens between me and another person, give me the courage to handle it quickly and in a way that pleases you, not in a selfish way.

- *But I tell you, love your enemies and pray for those who persecute you (Matthew 5:44, NIV).*

○   **What does it mean to me?**

It is easier to love the people that love you back. The challenge is not just to love my friends and family, but also my enemies and to even pray for the people who mistreat me. That is the power of God!

○   **Your quick prayer:**

God, teach me how to love my enemies! Help me to be patient with them and let my words be helpful, not harmful, to those that treat me wrong. I know revenge belongs to you so I will not get payback. I can treat my enemies well and show them your love because you still show me love when I hurt you and make bad choices.

❖ Exercise

• *For physical training is of some value, but godliness has value for all things, holding promise for both the present life and the life to come (1 Timothy 4:8, NIV).*

○   **What does it mean to me?**

Exercise has some benefits, but living in a way that pleases God makes everything good! Exercise keeps my body in shape, keeps me from getting certain diseases, keeps me focused in school, and makes sure I'm strong to run in the army of the Lord but too much exercise can also be unhealthy. It is all about balance. Living holy can never be excessive, if I walk in the love of God and keep the promises of God in my heart!

o **Your quick prayer:**

Father, thank you for this body that you have made. Teach me how to take care of my body by exercising, eating healthy things, drinking water, and getting enough sleep. But please, also show me how to take care of my spirit by reading my Bible, praying to you, fasting, and worshipping you so I can grow closer to you!

F

❖ **Family**

- *Don't let anyone look down on you because you are young, but set an example for the believers in speech, in conduct, in love, in faith and in purity (1 Timothy 4:12, NIV).*

  ○ **What does it mean to me?**

    Even though I am young, I am supposed to set an example to my loved ones on how to speak, behave, love, and believe in Christ. I am not too young to be an example of Christ's love.

  ○ **Your quick prayer:**

    Heavenly Father, I need your Spirit to teach me how to love my family and respect my parents. Teach them how to raise me, as a teenager, and show me how to honor them so we can work together in the kingdom. Then please teach me how I can be an example to my family about how to walk in your love and Spirit.

- *Honor your father and your mother, as the LORD your God has commanded you, so that you may live long and that it may go well with you in the land the LORD your God is giving you (Deuteronomy 5:16, NIV).*

  - **What does it mean to me?**

    God has instructed me to listen and respect my father and mother so that I can live a long life and so that he will bless me in the good things he has prepared for me.

  - **Your quick prayer:**

    Heavenly father, I need your Spirit to teach me how to love and respect my parents. I want to have a long life and be blessed so show me how to honor my parents even when I disagree with them. I need your help the most when we disagree so help me to obey your command and make you smile.

❖ Fasting

- *But when you fast, put oil on your head and wash your face, so that it will not be obvious to others that you are fasting, but only to your Father, who is unseen; and your Father, who sees what is done in secret, will reward you (Matthew 6:17-18, NIV).*

○ **What does it mean to me?**

When I fast, or deny something, to get closer to God I should not walk around looking sad and obvious. Fasting should be between me and God. It's my way of denying my flesh to get closer to God. When I fast in secret God sees my sacrifice and will bless me because I actually sacrificed something to show that I love and want to be closer to him.

○ **Your quick prayer:**

God, thank you for being with me when I fast. I desire to be near you and am willing to turn away _____ (whatever you are sacrificing like food, TV, radio, social media, etc.) to get closer to you. Please meet me and fill me with your Spirit so I can shine brightly around everyone I meet.

❖ Fighting

• *You desire but do not have, so you kill. You covet but you cannot get what you want, so you quarrel and fight. You do not have because you do not ask God (James 4:2, NIV).*

○ **What does it mean to me?**

I desire certain things or want to be heard so I argue and fight with people, but as a child of God I do not have certain things because I have not asked him for it. I should focus on my source, which is God, not fighting with others. God knows what I need and will provide for my need when it is time.

- ○ **Your quick prayer:**

    Heavenly Father, you are my shepherd I shall not want. You have good plans for me, and because I know you have good plans for me I will not waste my energy on things that destroy my witness as a kingdom kid, or that only please my flesh. Let my words and actions be pleasing in your sight.

- *Therefore I do not run like someone running aimlessly; I do not fight like a boxer beating the air (1 Corinthians 9:26,* NIV*).*

    - ○ **What does it mean to me?**

        Because I am a kingdom kid I have to go into training because my salvation is about staying strong until the end, like in a race. So I cannot waste my energy on things that don't matter in the big picture of my life. Fighting with people is like beating the air, pointless and just wastes my energy. The battle belongs to my God.

○ **Your quick prayer:**

> Jesus, I do believe that I am in training as a kingdom kid to stay strong in my faith and represent the kingdom well! Lord, I know that you can help me see what does or does not matter so I do not waste my energy fighting temporary fights! I have too many other good things to do to live just any way.

❖ Fingering

- *I have the right to do anything, you say—but not everything is beneficial. I have the right to do anything"—but not everything is constructive (1 Corinthians 10:23,* NIV*).*

    ○ **What does it mean to me?**

    > Even if fingering is not against the law, everything is not good for me. Everything that feels good at the time is not good for me in the end. A temporary pleasure can lead to lasting hurt or embarrassment.

    ○ **Your quick prayer:**

    > Father, grant me clear thoughts so that I do not do things that would make you disappointed. When people try to persuade me to do sexual things I need your courage to know that I am

worth the wait and that even though it is not illegal or sex, it is still violating my body, which is your temple, where your Spirit lives.

- *The eyes of the LORD are everywhere, keeping watch on the wicked and the good. (Proverbs 15:3, NIV).*

  - **What does this mean to me?**

    Even if nobody is around, God sees everything. The same way God knows when to come to my rescue is the same way that he knows when I am making a bad decision. I cannot hide from God.

  - **Your quick prayer:**

    Father, please help me to be clear in my thoughts so that I do not do things that are not good for me. I will choose to live for you even when nobody else is watching because you see everything. Even though this is not sex, I will not try to fool you by doing other sexual things.

❖ Friendship

- *Two are better than one, because they have a good return for their labor: If either of them falls down, one can help the other up. But pity anyone who falls and has no one to help them up (Ecclesiastes 4:9-10, NIV).*

○ **What does this mean to me?**

Having a friend or a partner is better than being alone because when you both work together you get more done. Also, if one of you falls or has a hard time, the friend can help the other friend. But having a hard time when you are alone is difficult to get out of.

○ **Your quick prayer:**

Father, thank you for my friends. Thank you for giving me someone to help me, listen to me, and show me love. Bless me to bless my friends and show them your love everyday.

G

❖ Gossip

- *And to make it your ambition to lead a quiet life: You should mind your own business and work with your hands, just as we told you (1 Thessalonians 4:11, NIV).*

  - **What does this mean to me?**

    Make it my business to live in peace with people, focus on my life and mind my business. Instead of talking about other people's lives even if it's a true story, I should focus on making my life better. Even if I am just sharing a true story about what happened in somebody's life it is still gossiping.

  - **Your quick prayer:**

    Father, teach me how to focus on myself and making my life better. Teach me how to live at peace with people as much as I can and to mind my own business. When somebody begins to bring up other people's business, Holy Spirit teach me the right words to say to change the conversation into something positive.

❖ Grades

- *Even small children are known by their actions, so is their conduct really pure and upright? (Proverbs 20:11, NIV).*

  - ○ **What does this mean to me?**

    Even young people, including me, are known by how they behave. This includes my grades and how I behave at home and school. Is my behavior really pure and right, or could I do better to be a light for my teachers and classmates?

  - ○ **Your quick prayer:**

    Even though I am young I will let my shine in my school. I will do my homework, class work, and participate so people can see you through me! When I feel overwhelmed, God show me how to manage my time every day to keep me from making bad decisions and going on the wrong path.

❖ Grief

- *There is a time for everything, and a season for every activity under the heavens:...a time to weep and a time to laugh, a time to mourn and a time to dance (Ecclesiastes 3:1; 4, NIV).*

○ **What does this mean to me?**

Everything in life has a time and a reason. When someone that I love dies it is okay for me to be sad or grieve. God did promise to be near me when I am grieving a loved one. When things are going well it is okay for me to dance and celebrate!

○ **Your quick prayer:**

Father, you said you are near the broken hearted. My heart is heavy and I am sad because I miss _____. Jesus, be with me. You are my strength and I need you right now. I know you hear me. Thank you for caring for me. I can't make it without your love right now.

H

❖ Holiness

- *For it is written: "Be holy, because I am holy." (1 Peter 1:16, NIV).*
  - ○ **What does it mean to me?**

    Because I am a child of the King, and a part of the royal priesthood, there are certain things that have to change. I have to try to be like Christ in my actions and thinking so others can see that I belong to him. Being like Christ means being holy. Being holy means walking in love, following the Spirit of God, and living according to the word of God.

  - ○ **Your quick prayer:**

    I live in this world, God, but help me to show your love by following your commands. I know that your commands are to protect me and give me a great life. When it is time for me to make decisions help me remember that I am holy and have standards.

- *Do not conform to the pattern of this world, but be transformed by the renewing of your mind. Then you will be able to test and approve what God's will is—his good, pleasing and perfect will (Romans 12:2, NIV).*

  ○ **What does this mean to me?**

    Even though I am a teenager, I cannot do what everybody else in the world does. As a child of the King there are certain things I just will not do (smoke, drink, sex, lie, gossip, etc.), but I still can have a fun life!! I can stay strong by changing how I think, according to the Bible. If I get my mind right and follow God's instructions I can show people that God has good plans for them when they agree with him.

  ○ **Your quick prayer:**

    God, thank you for allowing good things to happen to me. Thank you for showing me that I am royalty and heirs with Jesus to the kingdom. As your child teach me how to balance having fun and keeping my standards.

❖ Homework

- *Whatever you do, work at it with all your heart, as working for the Lord, not for human masters (Colossians 3:23, NIV).*

  ○ **What does this mean to me?**

  Everything that I do (homework, class work, projects, chores, etc.) represents God so I should always do my best. In doing my homework, I must remember that how I live in this earth still should be to worship and please my God. I can't confess to be a follower of Christ and not handle my business in school or work. Everything I do is to bless you.

  ○ **Your quick prayer:**

  Father, sometimes there is a lot of homework and sometimes I do not want to do my homework, but I believe that you will grant me favor with my teachers and show me how to manage my schedule to get everything done. Let my homework come to me easily so that I can understand the concepts and help me learn in my classes so I can be educated and successful. With that success I will use every opportunity to share your goodness.

I

❖ Internet

- *I have the right to do anything, you say—but not everything is beneficial. I have the right to do anything"—but not everything is constructive (1 Corinthians 10:23, NIV).*

  - ### What does this mean to me?

    The internet is a great tool, but some things can also be dangerous. I have the right to be on the internet with homework, social media, etc. but I have to remember that there are some bad things on the internet too. Everything is not good.

  - ### Your quick prayer:

    Father, help me see what is good for me and what things I should stay away from. Keep me safe while on the internet and help me find the things I'm looking for on the internet. Block any people or things that would do me harm in Jesus's name.

❖ Interview

- *It is God who judges: He brings one down, he exalts another (Psalm 75:7, NIV).*

  ○ **What does this mean to me?**

    I can't put myself in a job or give myself a promotion. God is the one who closes or opens doors. I still have to try and present myself in a good way to interviews, but if it is for me God will open the door. I won't ever know if the job is for me unless I try.

  ○ **Your quick prayer:**

    Lord, promotion comes from you and you have ordered my steps. I know that I will never know what you have for me unless I walk by faith. Show me what to wear and remind me of my accomplishments to share with the interviewer. Be with me because only you brings one person down and raises up another person. Raise me up if this is your will for me!

J

❖ Jobs/ Chores

- *Whatever you do, work at it with all your heart, as working for the Lord, not for human masters (Colossians 3:23, NIV).*

  ○ **What does this mean to me?**

  Everything that I do is an opportunity to show the love and goodness of God. Everyone has a boss, but the ultimate boss is God. He watches everything, so everything that I do should be to make him smile. I can't confess to be a follower of Christ and not handle my business in school or work.

  ○ **Your quick prayer:**

  I can do everything through Christ that strengthens me. Everything I do represents you so help me to have the same attitude Christ did in doing my work everyday! Even when I am tired help me to have a positive attitude and be a good worker.

K

❖ Kindness

- *Love is patient, love is kind. It does not envy, it does not boast, it is not proud (1 Corinthians 13:4, NIV).*

  - ### What does this mean to me?

    If I claim to love someone that means that I show kindness to them! Not only am I kind, even when I don't feel like it, but I am patient and grateful for what I have and humble when I show love.

  - ### Your quick prayer:

    Your word says that people will know me by my fruit. Let my love be patient, kind, and humble. Even on my bad days, teach me kindness so that my emotions do not get the best of me. Let my words be helpful and not hurtful in every situation!

L

❖ Loneliness

- *Turn to me and be gracious to me, for I am lonely and afflicted (Psalm 25:16, NIV).*

    ○ **What does this mean to me?**

    This is a prayer for when I feel alone and in trouble. I need God to look at me and be with me.

    ○ **Your quick prayer:**

    God, I feel alone and in trouble. You said you would never leave me so I need to feel your presence like David did, so I know that I am not alone and that you love me.

❖ Love

- *If you love me, keep my commands (John 14:15, NIV).*

  - **What does this mean to me?**

    It is not enough just to tell God that I love him. Actions speak louder than words, so I prove my love for God by doing the things that he has asked me to do as his child- all of the time, not just when I feel like it.

  - **Your quick prayer:**

    Lord, I love you. Help me love you more each day and teach me how to show my love for you, Almighty God! I will do your word and not just hear it and forget about it. Thank you for loving me and showing me. I want my relationship with you to be constant and I'm willing to do my part.

M

❖ Money

- *For the love of money is a root of all kinds of evil. Some people, eager for money, have wandered from the faith and pierced themselves with many griefs (1 Timothy 6:10, NIV).*

  ○ **What does it mean to me?**

  I need money to survive in our world, but God already knows this. Loving money, being greedy, or overly hungry for money can lead me to making bad choices. Some people, because they were so hungry to get money, have actually walked away from their faith in God and caused themselves many problems.

  ○ **Your quick prayer:**

  The Lord is my Shepherd I will not want. You are the God that will supply all of my needs. The earth and everything in it belongs to you so I trust that you have everything planned in my life. I believe that money will come to me and that I will give back my tithe and offering knowing you will open the windows of heaven and pour out blessings I won't have room to receive.

- *Bring the whole tithe into the storehouse, that there may be food in my house. Test me in this," says the LORD Almighty, "and see if I will not throw open the floodgates of heaven and pour out so much blessing that there will not be room enough to store it (Malachi 3:10, NIV).*

  ○ **What does this mean to me?**

    God has asked that I bring ten percent of what I earn into the kingdom or church so there can be something to use to bless others and to keep the church running. Paying my tithe shows my faith, because I am obedient to what God has asked while believing that he will take care of me so much that I will not have enough room to keep it! I must remember that this blessing will not only be money, but could also be good health, safety or protection, better grades, favor with my teachers, and many other things because blessings are so big.

  ○ **Your quick prayer:**

    Lord, I thank you for what you have given me. I trust that my money can help keep the church going and bless others in need. Lord, thank you for keeping the devil off of my back and blessing me so much that I do not have enough room to store all of the good things you have for me.

- *The LORD is my shepherd, I lack nothing (Psalm 23:1, NIV).*

  ○ **What does this mean to me?**

    The Lord takes care of me, so I do not need to be desperate or want anything. He knows what I need and how to take care of me so I trust him to be my God.

  ○ **Your quick prayer:**

    The Lord is my shepherd I will not want for anything. Instead I will focus on thanking you for the things you have done for me and my family. You are the God that will supply all of my needs. When my eyes or my heart want something that is not for me right now, help me to wait until you release good things to me so I can handle them.

N

❖ Nosiness/ Nosey

- *And to make it your ambition to lead a quiet life: You should mind your own business and work with your hands, just as we told you (1 Thessalonians 4:11, NIV).*

  ○ **What does this mean to me?**

  Make it my business to live in peace with people, focus on my life, and mind my business. Instead of talking about other people's lives, I should focus on making my life better.

  ○ **Your quick prayer:**

  Father, thank you for all of the good things that have happened in my life. I thank you that you will bless my brothers and sisters in Christ. Show me how to mind my business and be the best me that I can be!

O

❖ Obedience

- *Slaves, obey your earthly masters in everything; and do it, not only when their eye is on you and to curry their favor, but with sincerity of heart and reverence for the Lord. (Colossians 3:22,* NIV*).*

  - **What does this mean to me?**

    Although I am not a slave, as a kingdom kid I obey and follow the rules of the people God has set in charge. This means my parents, pastor, teachers, police officers, etc. I am to obey not only when they are watching me and to get on their good side, but I am to obey their rules from my heart and to honor my God.

  - **Your quick prayer:**

    I love you, God. Thank you for the people that you have set up to teach me and help me grow into an even better person. Lord, help me to listen to the adults that are leading and raising me. Help me to do right even when they provoke me or do not treat me well and show me how to be a holy young person that makes you smile because I make good choices.

❖ Oral Sex (See *Sex*)

❖ Overweight

- *I praise you because I am fearfully and wonderfully made; your works are wonderful, I know that full well (Psalm 139:14, NIV).*

  - ○ **What does this mean to me?**

    I praise God because he made me and set apart. I know that God makes wonderful things including me, just the way that I am.

  - ○ **Your quick prayer:**

    Father, please help me to remember that you made me just the way that I am! Despite everything around me you knew me and formed me in my mom's belly to be just who I am. Thank you for making me precious in your eyes!

- *Do you not know that your bodies are temples of the Holy Spirit, who is in you, whom you have received from God? You are not your own (1 Corinthians 6:19, NIV).*

○ **What does this mean to me?**

My body is a temple for the Holy Spirit, who I received from God. I belong to God, so I should take care of my body to protect it from illness by getting proper sleep, eating nutritionally, exercising my body, and challenging my mind.

○ **Your quick prayer:**

Father, thank you for this body that you have made. Thank you for loving me just the way that I am. I want to take care of this temple because you have trusted me with your Holy Spirit so please show me how to take care of this body so I can continue to grow stronger and smarter.

P

❖ Pornography

- *I have the right to do anything, you say—but not everything is beneficial. I have the right to do anything"—but not everything is constructive (1 Corinthians 10:23, NIV).*

  - **What does this mean to me?**

    Pornography is not illegal, but it is not helpful to me or my relationship with God. Looking at something that does not encourage things the way God set them up is not edifying to me nor is it worth the trouble I could get into.

  - **Your quick prayer:**

    Father, help me to keep my eyes pure and from watching things that would only bring me away from you. When I have the desire to look at pornography, show me how to replace the thoughts with something that is from you.

❖ Pray/ Prayer

- *Pray continually (1 Thessalonians 5:17, NIV).*
    - **What does this mean to me?**

        I can pray or talk to God all the time. It can be a silent prayer, in my head, or out loud but talking to God is important so I can keep a relationship with him. God has called me his friend. I talk to my friends all of the time, so I should talk to God all the time too—about decisions, good things, bad things, my emotions, events happening, etc.

    - **Your quick prayer:**

        Father, show me how to pray continually. Help me begin to talk to you with every decision I make—from the clothes I wear to the classes I should take and even how to respond in different situations. Teach me how you created me to pray and let me not be ashamed about how I spend time with you or get to know you!

❖ Pressure

- *Do not be anxious about anything, but in every situation, by prayer and petition, with thanksgiving, present your requests to God. And the peace of God, which transcends all understanding, will guard your hearts and your minds in Christ Jesus (Philippians 4:6-7,* NIV*).*

○ **What does this mean to me?**

I do not need to be anxious or feel pressured for anything. Instead, I can talk to God and give him thanks while asking him what I need. Then God will grant me his peace to protect my heart and mind in Christ Jesus.

○ **Your quick prayer:**

Father, you know everything that I need and even the things that I want. I thank you for loving me enough to know what I need and listening to me when I need help. Lord, I need help with _____ (fill in your issue here) and I know that you have already overcome everything in this world. So I receive your peace and trust that you are with me in this situation. Show me the way to get through this issue.

Q

❖ Quiet/ Being Quiet

- *I praise you because I am fearfully and wonderfully made; your works are wonderful, I know that full well (Psalm 139:14, NIV).*

  - ### What does this mean to me?

    I praise God because even though people say I am quiet, God gave me this gift of quietness for a reason. He made me perfectly and wonderfully and I do not need to change.

  - ### Your quick prayer:

    Father, thank you for making me how I am! Help me find what purpose my quietness serves and teach me how to serve others just the way I am. Lord I thank you that you will remind me that I am special and that I am perfect the way that I am because you made me!

R

❖ Relationships

- *A friend loves at all times, and a brother is born for adversity (Proverbs 17:17,* NIV*).*

  - **What does it mean to me?**

    My friends are always there and my brother or family is here to help me get through the rough times.

  - **Your quick prayer:**

    Father, thank you for the good relationships that I have. Show me how to be a good friend and family member. Let my words encourage my loved ones and help me to be a truth teller so my loved ones can rely on me. In the tough times show me to speak up if I need help and to communicate so that we can continue to grow in our relationship!

❖ Respect

- *Give to everyone what you owe them: If you owe taxes, pay taxes; if revenue, then revenue; if respect, then respect; if honor, then honor (Romans 13:7, NIV).*

  ○ **What does this mean to me?**

  I should do what I'm supposed to do. I represent the kingdom so I should give people what I owe them (honor or respect for teacher or parents, taxes to the government, money I borrow, homework to teachers, etc.).

  ○ **Your quick prayer:**

  Father, I want to show people what your love and truth are. Let me do this by being an example of keeping my word and doing what I say I'm going to do! Teach me to respect people when it is easy and even when it is difficult because it is all about shining brightly as a light!

❖ Rest

- *Come to me, all you who are weary and burdened, and I will give you rest (Matthew 11:28, NIV).*

○ **What does this mean to me?**

Jesus says I can come to him when I am feeling tired, stressed, or overwhelmed for help.

○ **Your quick prayer:**

Father, you are my safe place. I am tired and feeling stressed. Show me how to lean on you when I am feeling stressed or tired. I know that you are with me and will guide me in how to deal with everything in my life.

❖ Rumors

• *Do not spread false reports. Do not help a guilty person by being a malicious witness (Exodus 23:1, NIV).*

○ **What does this mean to me?**

I should not spread rumors or talk about people. When I share stories about other people I am helping people mistreat others.

○ **Your quick prayer:**

Father, I need courage to be quiet about things that are not about me. When people are gossiping and spreading rumors help me to stand up for what is right! Let my light shine so others can see that we should love and not hurt each other.

S

❖ Saved/Salvation

- *If you declare with your mouth, "Jesus is Lord," and believe in your heart that God raised him from the dead, you will be saved (Romans 10:9, NIV).*

  ○ **What does it mean to me?**

  If I say out of my mouth that Jesus is Lord and believe that God used his power to raise him from the dead after he died on the cross I will receive salvation.

  ○ **Your quick prayer:**

  Thank you, God, for sending Jesus to sacrifice his life for me. I believe that Jesus is Lord and that you raised him from the dead and that he is now in heaven with you. I ask that you teach me how to live life as a kingdom kid that belongs to you. I love you! Amen.

❖ School

- *Whatever you do, work at it with all your heart, as working for the Lord, not for human masters (Colossians 3:23, NIV).*

  ○ **What does it mean to me?**

  Everything that I do is an opportunity to show the love and goodness of God. Everyone has a boss, but the ultimate boss is God. He watches everything so everything that I do should be to make him smile and to represent the heavenly kingdom! I can't confess to be a follower of Christ and not handle my business in school. That means doing all of my work, on time, and being responsible.

  ○ **Your quick prayer:**

  I can do everything through Christ that strengthens me. Everything I do represents you so help me to have the same attitude Christ did in doing my school work, homework, projects, and being a student and classmate! Even when I am tired, help me to have a positive attitude and be a good worker.

❖ Self Esteem (See *Confidence*)

❖ Self Harm

❖ Sex

- *It is God's will that you should be sanctified: that you should avoid sexual immorality (1 Thessalonians 4:3, NIV).*

  ○ **What does this mean to me?**

    It is God's way that I should be holy or set apart and that I should stay away from anything sexually inappropriate like sex of any kind, or even things that lead to sex until I get married.

  ○ **Your quick prayer:**

    Lord, I want to be holy, so when temptation comes, help me to take the way of escape that you give me. Grant me courage to look for your help and to avoid situations that make it easy for me to make bad decisions.

❖ Sexting

- *But among you there must not be even a hint of sexual immorality, or of any kind of impurity, or of greed, because these are improper for God's holy people (Ephesians 5:3, NIV).*

  ○ **What does it mean to me?**

    I am God's special and set apart people! That means that I should stay away from anything sexually impure, like sex, things that lead to sex, or anything impure or greedy. Sexting is sharing my special body parts with someone when I should be saving those good things for my husband or wife. As God's holy people, I have a standard and I will represent the kingdom with how I live!

○ **Your quick prayer:**

Lord, I want to be holy, so when temptation comes help me to take the way of escape that you give me. Grant me courage to look for your help and to avoid situations that make it easy for me to make bad decisions.

• *I have the right to do anything, you say—but not everything is beneficial. I have the right to do anything"—but not everything is constructive (1 Corinthians 10:23,* NIV*).*

○ **What does this mean to me?**

Nudes or sexting is considered distributing or sharing child pornography and is against the law, so it is not a good idea to send pictures to others because it is illegal. A temporary picture can lead me to a long time of trouble.

○ **Your quick prayer:**

Father, please help me to be clear in my thinking so that I do not do things that are bad for me. When people try to persuade me to do sexual things, I need your courage to know that I am worth the wait. Even though it is not sex, it is still violating my body and your temple, where your Spirit lives, and breaking the law.

❖ Suicide

- *Though I walk in the midst of trouble, you preserve my life; you stretch out your hand against the wrath of my enemies, and your right hand delivers me (Psalm 138:7, NIV).*

  ◦ **What does this mean to me?**

    Around me there is trouble. Even though there is trouble around me, God will keep my life. He cares enough about me to stretch out his hand against the people and things that try to do me harm and take care of me. I have to trust him to make it.

  ◦ **Your quick prayer:**

    Father, I am in trouble. I do not want to live anymore. This is too much for me. You said you would keep my life so I need you to come to my rescue and help me to live! Show me who to go to when I am feeling badly, show me what to think about, show me how things will get better!

- *When you pass through the waters, I will be with you; and when you pass through the rivers, they will not sweep over you. When you walk through the fire, you will not be burned; the flames will not set you ablaze (Isaiah 43:2, NIV).*

  ○ **What does this mean to me?**

    When I go through tough things and feel like I am drowning God will be with me! I am not alone! When I go through hard things, I do not have to be overwhelmed. When I go through things that make me feel hurt or troubled, I will not die. I can remember that to make it, I have to keep going. God will show me the way. I will not die.

  ○ **Your quick prayer:**

    Father, I am in trouble. I do not want to live anymore. This is too much for me. You said you would keep my life so I need you to come to my rescue and help me to live! Show me who to go to when I am feeling badly, show me what to think about, show me how things will get better! I cannot do this alone and you told me that you would be with me so I need you. Help me.

Weekly Schedule

SUNDAY
- visit grandma
- attend mass

MONDAY
- dentist appointment

TUESDAY
- buy gift for Dad's birthday

WEDNESDAY
Piano practice

THURSDAY
- babysit niece
- math tutor

FRIDAY
Piano recital

SATURDAY
- clean room
- do homework

T

❖ Time Management

- *His master said to him, 'Well done, good and faithful servant. You have been faithful over a little; I will set you over much. Enter into the joy of your master (Matthew 25:21, NIV).*

  ○ **What does this mean to me?**

    In the Bible, when a worker showed his boss the work he completed, his boss gave him a compliment. The worker had been good at managing his time so the boss gave him a promotion. When I do well managing my time and getting important things done, it makes my Heavenly Father happy and shows that I can use my time well.

  ○ **Your quick prayer:**

    Heavenly father, teach me how to budget my time. Show me how to balance everything that I have to use my time wisely. If there are things to get rid of in my daily schedule, show me. If there are things I need to do, please show me. I just need you to show me how to use every minute you give me to live!

❖ Timing

- *A person finds joy in giving an apt reply— and how good is a timely word (Proverbs 15:23, NIV)!*

  ○ **What does this mean to me?**

    When someone says the right thing at the right time it is a great thing! Saying something that will help someone is a good thing, so I should think about that the words that come out of my mouth.

  ○ **Your quick prayer:**

    Let the words of my mouth and the thoughts of my heart please you. Oh Lord, you are my strength and my helper! Let my words help and not hurt others.

U

❖ Unholy

- *People will be lovers of themselves, lovers of money, boastful, proud, abusive, disobedient to their parents, ungrateful, unholy (2 Timothy 3:2, NIV).*

  ○ **What does this mean to me?**

    The Bible spoke about people having certain ways that don't please God. Loving myself or money more than God, thinking I'm the best in everything, being rude and hurtful to others, disobeying my parents, not being thankful, and acting just like everyone that is not saved is unholy and disappoints God.

  ○ **Your quick prayer:**

    Lord, you are holy. I am your child so teach me how to be holy! Create in me a clean heart and renew a right spirit within me!

❖ Unique

- *But you are a chosen people, a royal priesthood, a holy nation, God's special possession, that you may declare the praises of him who called you out of darkness into his wonderful light (1 Peter 2:9, NIV).*

  - **What does this mean to me?**

    I am chosen by God, I have royal duties, I am holy, and God's special people! We share in praising God and live a life that is unique and different. Because I am a Kingdom Kid I am unique and different, and it is okay!

  - **Your quick prayer:**

    God, I belong to you! I am unique and special! Help me remember that I am set apart for serving you! Thank you, Jesus, for giving me an abundant life! I will live my life remembering that I am yours and when I forget who I am, remind me that I belong to you!

❖ Upset

- *Be angry and do not sin; do not let the sun go down on your anger (Ephesians 4:26, NIV).*

○ **What does this mean to me?**

It is okay for me to be upset or angry, but I cannot use my feelings as an excuse to sin and make bad choices. I cannot keep my anger or being upset for long, because I do not want to give the enemy a chance to use my emotions as a way to mess up my relationships.

○ **Your quick prayer:**

Let the words of my mouth and the thoughts of my heart please you. Father, help me to forgive others just as you have forgiven me when I made poor choices. I won't let the enemy use me to create drama or problems.

V

❖ Vanity/ Vain

- *Yet when I surveyed all that my hands had done and what I had toiled to achieve, everything was meaningless [vain], a chasing after the wind; nothing was gained under the sun (Ecclesiastes 2:11, NIV).*

    ○ **What does this mean to me?**

    King Solomon was looking at everything he achieved and realized that out of all of the big things he worked so hard for there was always something else to be done. Even when I look at everything that I have done, in the big picture of life, there is always something else to be done. It's like chasing after the wind, I can't ever really catch the wind—I just keep trying. That is why I do things unto God because he sees my efforts and heart.

    ○ **Your quick prayer:**

    Father, I know that how I live represents the kingdom. Please help me to focus on what really matters in life. There is always something to reach for and always something that needs to be done, but I need your spirit of revelation and wisdom to seek your kingdom and do things to give you glory so it is not in vain or for nothing!

❖ Victim

- *You intended to harm me, but God intended it for good to accomplish what is now being done, the saving of many lives (Genesis 50:20 NIV).*

  ○ **What does this mean to me?**

  People will want to do bad things to me, but God will use the same "bad" thing to bless me. Not only will he use my bad situation to bless me, but he will also use it to bless others!

  ○ **Your quick prayer:**

  Thank you that everything that happens to me works together for my good! Help me to have courage, confidence, and wait on you to change the bad into a blessing! I am trusting you even though I don't like this place I'm in. Thank you for being my help when I need you!

W

❖ **War**

- *Praise be to the LORD my Rock, who trains my hands for war, my fingers for battle (Psalm 144:1, NIV).*

  ○ **What does this mean to me?**

  I thank God because he is my safe place and teaches me how to fight in the kingdom. He shows me what strategies to use when I am in battle against the enemy and forces of darkness so I can have victory.

  ○ **Your quick prayer:**

  Father, I know that I am more than a conqueror through Jesus! I know that you have my back and will teach me how to war and fight the good fight of faith!

❖ Work

- *Whatever you do, work at it with all your heart, as working for the Lord, not for human masters (Colossians 3:23, NIV).*

  ○ **What does this mean to me?**

    Everything that I do is an opportunity to show the love and goodness of God. Everyone has a boss, but you are the ultimate boss! I know you watch everything so everything that I do should be to make you smile and to represent the heavenly kingdom! I can't confess to be a follower of Christ and not do my best at my job. That means doing all of my work, on time, and being responsible and respectful to my boss.

  ○ **Your quick prayer:**

    I can do everything through Christ that strengthens me. Everything I do represents you so help me to have the same attitude Christ did in doing my work and being a coworker! Even when I am tired, help me to have a positive attitude and be a good worker to bring you glory!

❖ Worship

- *God is spirit, and his worshipers must worship in the Spirit and in truth (John 4:24, NIV).*

  ○ **What does this mean to me?**

    God is spirit so I may not seem him, but he is there! As a kingdom kid, I must worship God from my heart by being honest with him when I praise him and talk with him.

  ○ **Your quick prayer:**

    Lord! I know that you are spirit so help me seek you and your kingdom, not just for when I need things! I want to love you and get to know you, so I ask that you walk with me and help me worship you from my heart and actions, not just with my words!

X

❖ X-Rated things

- *The beginning of wisdom is this: Get wisdom. Though it cost all you have, get understanding (Proverbs 4:7, NIV).*

    - **What does this mean to me?**

        Even though I am young, I should be wise in the situations I am in. This includes being smart about what I expose myself to (movies, music, etc.) and the environments I put myself in because I am a witness for Christ and I can't take God's temple (my body) just anywhere because God is holy.

    - **Your quick prayer:**

        Heavenly father, your word said I can ask for wisdom and that you would give it freely to me so I am asking for wisdom with where I go, what I look at, and what I listen to. Help me to shine brightly anywhere that I go for your praise and help me to avoid temptation as much as I can!

Y

❖ Yell/Yelling

- *A gentle answer turns away wrath, but a harsh word stirs up anger (Proverbs 15:1, NIV).*

  - ### What does this mean to me?

    Giving someone a gentle or calm response helps to stop wrath and arguments, but loud responses can bring more anger and yelling.

  - ### Your quick prayer:

    Father, show me how to give a calm answer so I can stop this argument. Put a guard on my mouth so that I represent you with how I respond.

❖ Young/ Youth

- *Don't let anyone look down on you because you are young, but set an example for the believers in speech, in conduct, in love, in faith and in purity (1 Timothy 4:12, NIV).*

  ○ **What does it mean to me?**

  Even though I am young, I am supposed to set an example to other believers on how to speak, behave, love, and believe in Christ. I am not too young to be an example of Christ's love.

  ○ **Your quick prayer:**

  Heavenly father, I need your spirit to teach me how to be an example. I am young and have strength so help me to use my youth to serve others. I receive your love and just ask that you teach me how to live abundantly every day and show others your truth and love with how I live my life!

Z

❖ **Zeal**

- *Desire without knowledge is not good—how much more will hasty feet miss the way (Proverbs 19:2, NIV)*

  ○ **What does it mean to me?**

    Having zeal or excitement about God without being educated from the word of God and the kingdom of God is not good because I can make the wrong decisions in my excitement.

  ○ **Your quick prayer:**

    Father, I love you and want to live for you! I commit myself to you and ask that you help me read my word so that I can know what you want from me as your child, all of the good things you have for me, and how the devil will try to do me harm. Help me to make time to spend with you so I can learn and remember who I am in you and so I can make good decisions based on your word!

ARE THERE ANY other words that you need that were left out? Write them on this page and remember to study and think about God's word because that is the only way that we stay holy in our society! God is with you, but you have to work out your salvation and tough stuff every day!

_____

_____

_____

_____

_____

_____

_____

_____

_____

_____

_____

_____

_____

_____

_____

_____

_____

_____

_____

_____

_____

_____

_____

www.ingramcontent.com/pod-product-compliance
Lightning Source LLC
Chambersburg PA
CBHW071121260626
47162CB00006B/2413